# AMIGOS

## Friends Forever

Stories and Pictures by WALKO

Sky Pony Press
New York

One day, Pedro was feeling cooped up at home, so he went out into the great wide world. He wanted to experience something new, wanted to smell new aromas, hear new sounds, and learn new things. He sniffed a bit here, and sniffed a bit there, and was feeling good.

Soon Pedro came to a street. Carrramba!! A car nearly ran him over!

"Careful, muchacho!" someone shouted.

"Don't you have any eyes in your head?"

"Of course I do!" Pedro cried back.

"I just can't see anything with them!"

That's because Pedro had been blind since birth.

"My name is Pedro. And you are?" he asked.

"Hola! My name is Rosalie and I am pleased to meet you!" said Rosalie, coming slowly out from behind the bush.

"You have a beautiful voice," said Pedro."What are you waiting for over here?"

"I want to cross the street, just like you. I want to head out into the wide world," said Rosalie.

"But with my lame leg, I'm too slow and could easily be run over."

"Is it that dangerous?" asked Pedro.

"Ay, muchacho, you sure ask lots of questions!" exclaimed Rosalie. "Listen carefully!"

So Rosalie described the big heavy buses, the fast cars, and all the other vehicles that thundered along the road there.

Pedro could hear everything of course, but he couldn't see it.

"Caramba!" he cried. Never in his life had someone taught him so many important things! And Rosalie's voice was so enchanting!

Rosalie thought talking to Pedro was nice too,
since Pedro was very good at listening. Never before
had she met such an attentive listener!

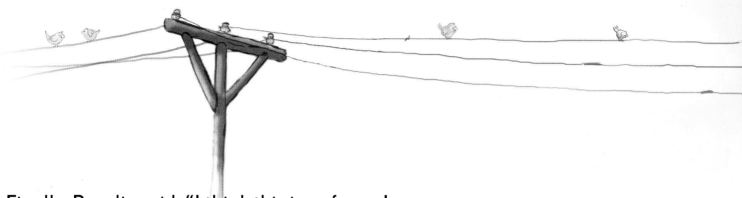

Finally, Rosalie said, "I think this is as far as I can go. But you have fast legs, so I'll keep an eye out for you and give you a sign when you can cross the street safely."

"Caramba, that's really nice of you, Rosalie," said Pedro. "But let's think of a way for us both to get to the other side instead!"

And he lay down in the grass to think. Rosalie did the same. They thought and thought—the entire afternoon. Pedro and Rosalie weren't exactly quick thinkers.

But just as the sun started to set, Pedro made a sudden leap into the air! He had the perfect idea!

"I've got it, Rosalie," he cried loudly.

"Huh!?" Rosalie asked, startled.

"You'll be our eyes and I'll run for us," Pedro laughed.

"Huuuuuuuh...?" Rosalie asked again. She was worried that Pedro had suddenly lost his mind.

"Are you all right, muchacho?" she asked.

"Si, Señorita," said Pedro, which means something like "Yes, little miss."

Then he lifted Rosalie onto his broad shoulders in a flash. The idea was quite simple: Rosalie looked left and right and then left and right again. And when the road was clear she called out:

"Rápido, muchacho!"

Then Pedro galloped as fast as he could straight across the road, and in no time at all they had safely reached the other side.

You know, that's just how things are with good ideas. The good ones are always the simplest...

Now their path to the wide-open world was clear again, and it was time to say goodbye.

"It has been a great pleasure for me, dear Rosalie," said Pedro. "I wish you the best of luck. Hopefully we'll meet again! Hasta la vista!"

And Rosalie said, "It was very nice to meet you. Hasta la vista, and take good care of yourself, amigo!"

Amigo means friend, and so they hugged each other tightly goodbye, as friends do.

Then they each went on their way, just as they had planned.

But when they had gone just a few steps, they suddenly both felt very strange. Pedro already missed Rosalie. And all at once, Rosalie thought life was terribly lonely without Pedro.

So Rosalie called out to Pedro, "Amigo, why don't we travel the world together? Then we won't be alone!"

"Oh yes, that would be nice!" Pedro called back. "I'll run for us and you'll see for us! And we can talk and have fun!"

From then on, Rosalie and Pedro traveled the world together for the rest of their lives.

Nothing could stop them, because they were friends and they stuck together like glue.

Rosalie's eyes saw for them both, and Pedro's fast legs carried them wherever they wanted to go, every single day.

Hasta la vista, amigos!